Slumbery Stumb in the Jungle

Written and illustrated by Sarah McConnell

Colour by Paloma Pedrera Martinez

Collins

One evening, in the big green jungle, a gentle breeze blew through the leaves. Monkey was still awake. He'd spent all day trying to tell his friends something important, but they wouldn't listen.

"The forest is getting smaller," he said.
"A big yellow monster is coming."

"Monkey is always telling stories," said Giraffe to Rhino, shaking her head.

"Big yellow monster, how silly," laughed Rhino. "Monkey is scared of everything. He isn't even brave enough to swing out of his tree."

"Huh," said Monkey. "I'll show them."
He peered down at the ground,
but it was too far away.

"Maybe tomorrow," he thought,
flopping down on his branch.

Monkey closed his eyes and
a strange song, a distant
brum-brum, lulled him to sleep.

Suddenly, Monkey stood up,
but his eyes were tightly shut.

"Look," Giraffe gasped.
"Monkey's sleepwalking.
What shall we do?"

Monkey slid down Giraffe's long neck.

He balanced on Rhino's nose.

Nothing could wake him, until ...

... a pair of bright lights shone through the trees.

"Where am I?" said Monkey in surprise. Then he heard it. A loud brum-brum noise.

“The big yellow monster!” shouted Monkey.

“He’s right,” Rhino cried, “but what can we do?”

Monkey knew. He had to get help.
But it meant swinging out of
the tree, all by himself.

"I can't do it," whispered Monkey, but the brum-brum noise was getting nearer and nearer.

He took a deep breath, then
leapt out into the jungle.

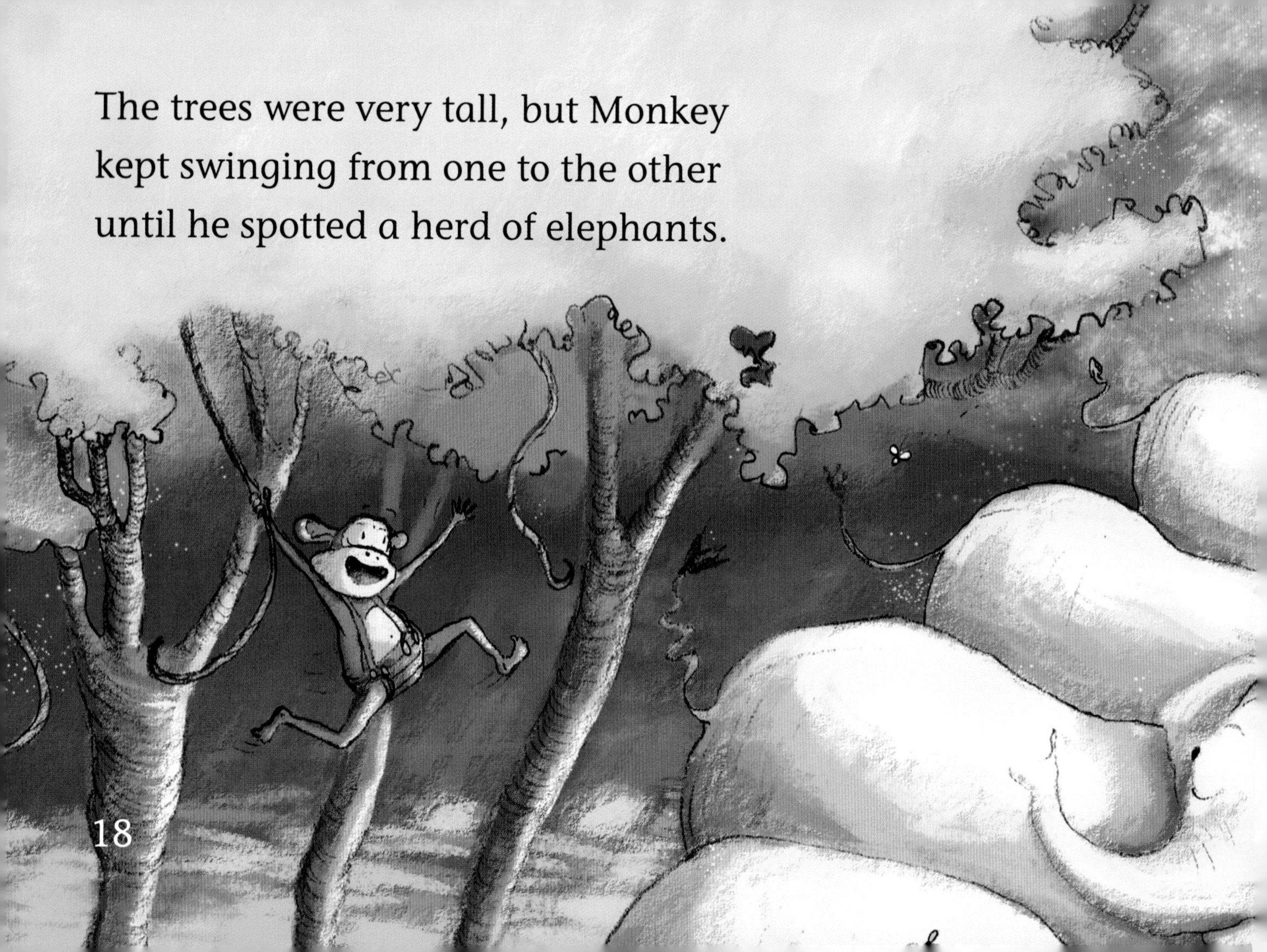

The trees were very tall, but Monkey kept swinging from one to the other until he spotted a herd of elephants.

Monkey told them what was happening. "Of course we'll help!" they said, getting together and galloping towards the bright lights.

"Big yellow monster, you're not so big now," shouted Monkey.

The monster screeched, turned and ran away.

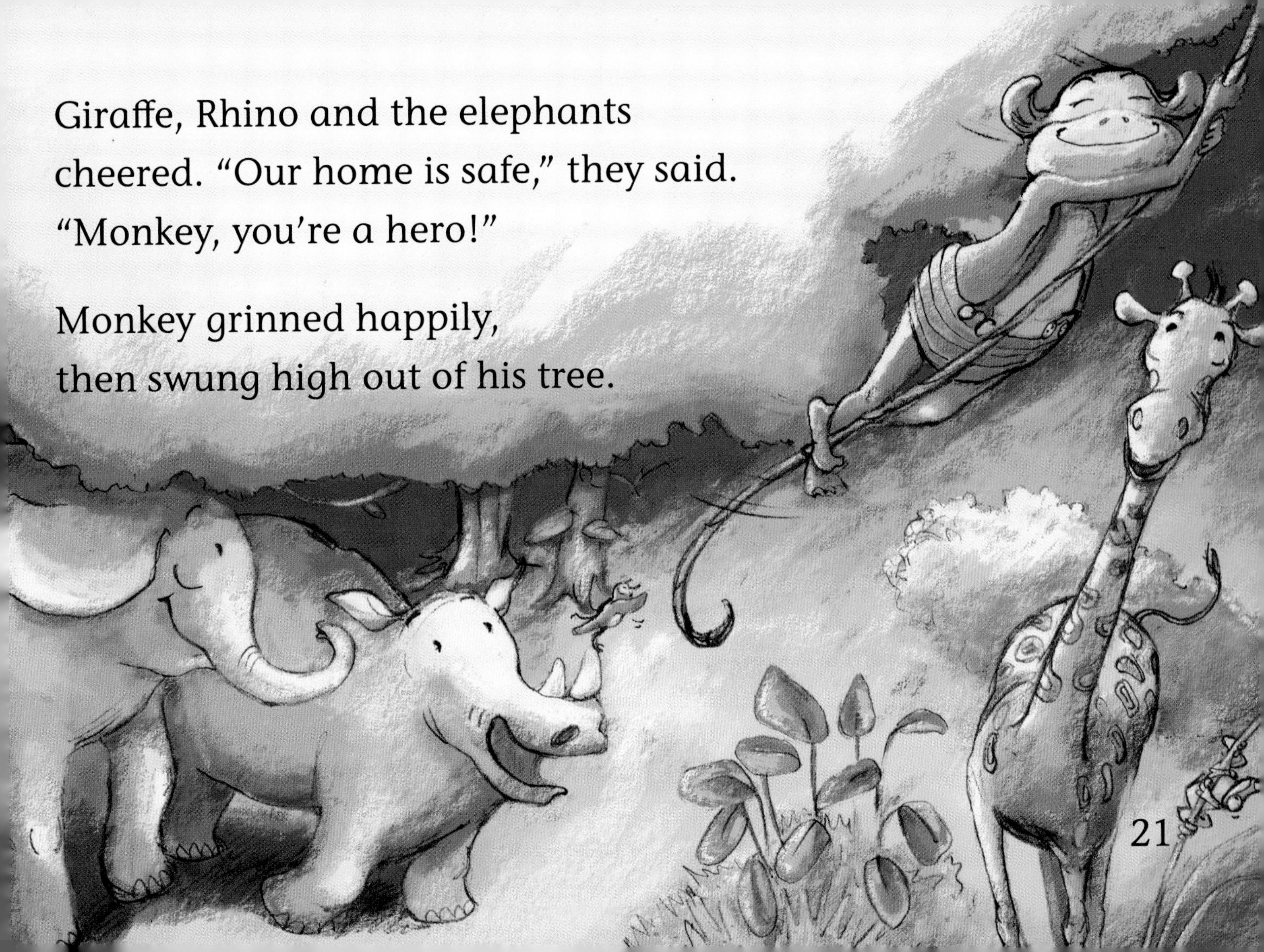

Giraffe, Rhino and the elephants cheered. "Our home is safe," they said. "Monkey, you're a hero!"

Monkey grinned happily, then swung high out of his tree.

How Monkey got swinging

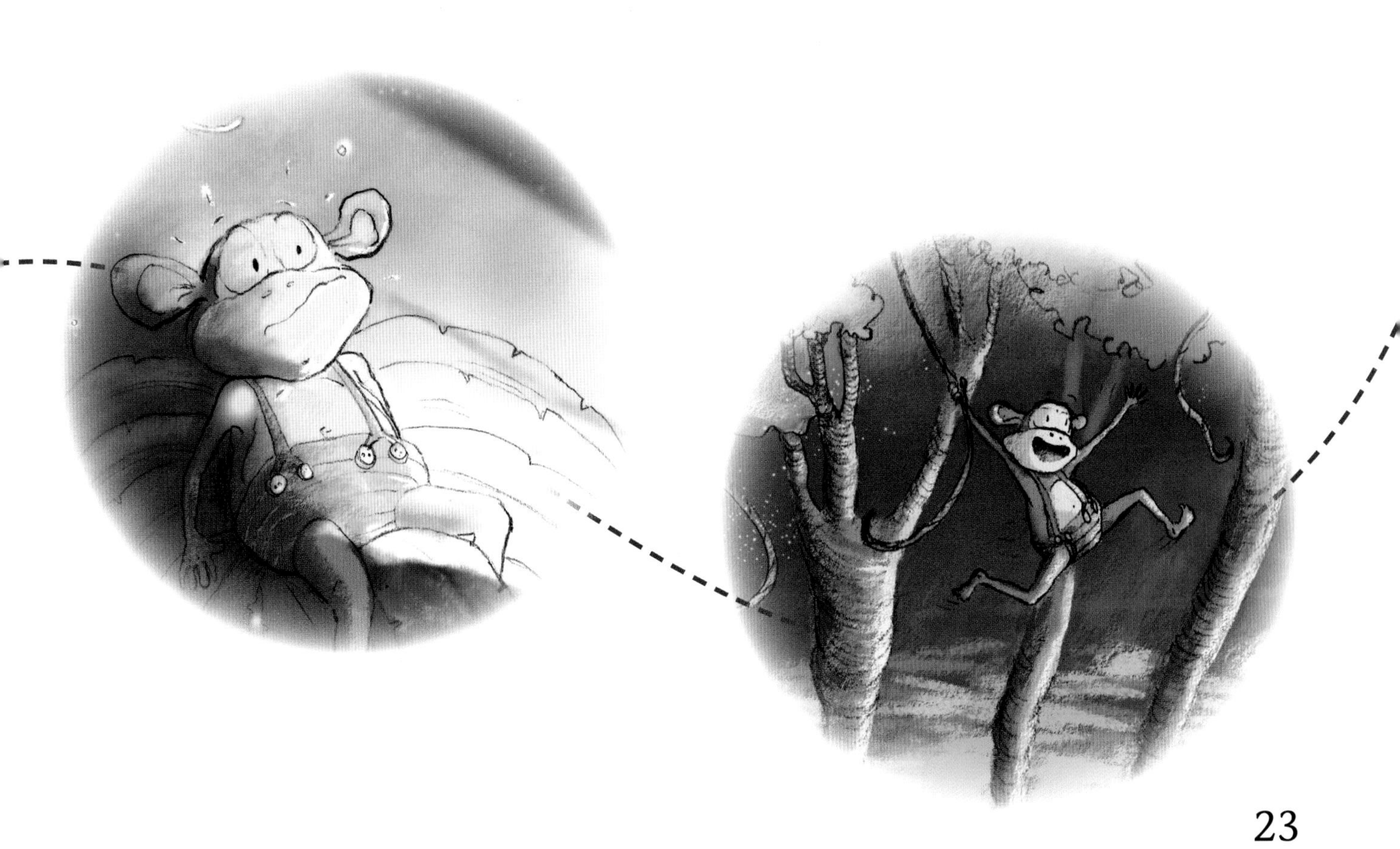

Ideas for reading

Written by Gillian Howell
Primary Literacy Consultant

Reading objectives:
- discuss word meanings, link new meanings to those already known
- make inferences on the basis of what is being said and done
- be encouraged to link what they read or hear read to their own experiences

Spoken language objectives:
- use spoken language to develop understanding through speculating, imagining and exploring ideas
- participate in discussions and role play
- give well-structured descriptions, explanations and narratives for different purposes, including for expressing feelings

Curriculum links: Geography; Science; Art

Interest words: slumbery, stumble, jungle, monkey, friends, monster, giraffe, rhino, elephants

Word count: 320

Resources: paper, pencils, crayons or paint, scissors, sticks or straws to make puppets

Build a context for reading

This book can be read over two or more reading sessions.

- Look together at the cover illustration. Ask the children to speculate on what the story might be about and where it is set. Ask the children to say what they think the monkey is doing and what other animals might live in this setting.
- Read the title together. Explain the meaning of "slumbery" and "stumble" and ask the children to suggest other words with similar meanings.
- Turn to the back and read the back cover blurb to confirm the children's predictions about the plot.

Understand and apply reading strategies

- Read pp2–3 together. Ask the children why they think Monkey was still awake.